T0078040

Joy, Joy, Joy

Teaching Your Child (and Yourself) to Have JOY - No Matter What

1st Edition

Elizabeth Wiley MA JD, Pomo Elder

 www.trafford.com
North America & international
toll-free: 844-688-6899 (USA & Canada)
fax: 812 355 4082

INTRODUCTION

Our books are written as on ongoing series for high risk youth, veterans, and first responders as well as their parents and those who are raising them.

One of the reasons for starting this series was we, as special needs teachers, as therapists, as Directors of programs and private schools for high risk youth began to recognize how many of the children and youth were children of veterans, grandchildren of veterans, and also first responders.

We then noticed the numbers of minority children and poverty level financial back grounds were the reality for high risk children and youth. We saw children of Mothers who had been as young as NINE at the birth of their child among the high risk students. Whether rich, or poverty level, we saw children of alcohol, sexual, and drug addictions.

We saw children as young as 18 months labeled with an alphabet of mental health disorders, medicated and put into "special schools" where in fact media found they were often warehoused, abused, and not taught at all. Upon seeing a news story about the schools discovered at some of the licensed sites, in which children and teens often did not have desks, or chairs to sit on, let alone proper educational supplies and equipment for special learning program, we joined with others, and designed programs.

We were naive enough to think our work, offered FREE in most cases, would be welcomed especially as we offer it free and often through research projects, but, it was NOT valued or wanted.

What? we asked?

We went back to college and while earning degrees we had apparently NOT needed while working with children of the very rich in expensive private schools, we did research projects to document our findings. To find ways to overcome the problems. Again, our work was NOT valued or wanted.

One of our associates, who had asked many of us to volunteer in a once a month FREE reading program in the local public schools, was held back for almost two years doing paperwork and proving her volunteers, most of them parents of successful children, teens and adults, could read a first five years book and teach parents how to read those books to their own children. She was a Deputy United States Prosecutor, and had recruited friends from all levels of law enforcement, child and family services, education and volunteer groups that served children and families.

None the less, we continued our work, met a fabulous and expensive Psychiatrist who was building his own server system and the first online education project after creating a massive and encompassing medical examination study guide for graduate medical students to assist them in passing global and national medical examinations for licensing.

We worked with a team of citizens and specialists in education who had created a 39 manual project for students, parents and teachers to be able to learn on their own.

This series of books includes ideas, history and thoughts from the students, the parents, and professionals who work with these situations.

Jesus was told, don't have children wasting your time, and he responded, let the children come.

Our work is to bring children to us, and to those who have the heart and love to develop the uniqueness and individuality of each of God's creations. Many of them are of different religions, and beliefs, and many are atheists but believe fully in the wonder and uniqueness of every human.

To all who have helped and continue to help children and anyone wanting to learn, we thank God and we thank you.

INTRODUCTION TO JOY

. . . .

JOY

What is it?

It is strength of self. To me it is learning EARLY to depend on GOD for calm, peace and courage in life, to be grateful for what is, the best we can, and to change things, to possess the calm and peace that need to be possessed to figure out what needs to be changed to make life better, for ourselves and others, and with God's help, to make the changes.

JOY

It is what keeps us from giving up and committing suicide when things are not so great, or when we try hard and still do not get things the way WE want them.

JOY

The ability to look at reality and figure it out.

Joy can be sitting in the bath tub, with bubbles and our rubber ducky, even if we are fifty and run our own business, are head of a family, or a teen that thinks all that angst will never end. Joy can be a seventy, eighty or ninety year old, hearing the voice of a great grandchild on the phone, receiving a drawing in crayon to put on the wall of the nursing home from a great-grandchild, no matter what losses injury, illness and age have brought. OR sitting with a hot bowl of bubble bath, hands in resting, rubber ducky bobbing along.

Sitting there for as long as it takes, crying if necessary, adding more hot water if needed until we are ready to get out and dry off and start on a new path. OR just go to bed and be ready to wake up in the morning with gratitude for something, even if it is just breathing.

Breathing is good, it means you are still living and can look for resolution to problems, and good things to have joy about.

JOY is also that feeling of seeing butterflies, or our favorite pet greet us after a long day of reality.

JOY is in all, gratitude to the Creator for all, no matter what.

How can we possible learn it, or teach it? Let's explore together!

Chapter One

. . . .

JOY

Getting Started

When a baby is born, do we greet that child with JOY.

Were we GRATEFUL even before the child is born and in our arms?

That feeling of JOY is going to transmit to the baby, before birth, and as it is clipped free of the natal cords and blood lines.

If we greet that child, wanted or unwanted at first, with JOY, our own feeling of JOY is going to be hardwired into the neurology of the child. This prenatal and natal caring and concern are subject of many research projects over the years of how attitude, music, and positive or negative stress change the neurological responses of the unborn.

SO, getting started starts BEFORE your child is even out in the air!

Chapter Two

. . . .

JOY, choosing to be Happy

Both President Lincoln, and First Lady Eleanor Roosevelt advised that we can be as happy as we choose.

Google both of these people, you will find what they each had to say about being happy being a choice.

You will find books that you can read that help you realize neither of them had lives that gave any reason for their steadfast commitment to joy, and helping others have an opportunity to find and enjoy JOY.

I've got the joy, joy, joy joy down in my heart. A children's religious song. Listen to several versions on You Tube with your children.

After World War II, hundreds of thousands of service men came home, with what today is called PTSD, or with severe injuries, or did not come home, hundreds of thousands had passed away. The families were often housed in old barracks, and Quonset hut villages while trying to figure out what to do. Many churches sent busses out to pick up the families for services.

After my parents divorced, we lived in an area where the bus came by. They taught the children to sing songs while on the bus ride to and from the church.

I've got the Joy, Joy, Joy, Joy, was one of those songs.

Today it is easy to find several versions of this song on You Tube.

In a time when families were hurting, that simple little song, and a ride to Sunday School and church events, such as all community repairs of homes needing it meant healing to hurting families or big community picnics at the beach or in some farmer's field, often dodging the giant cattle paddies (poop), or not! The people did NOT have to belong to the church, just be needing of a hand, or a day of church picnics, which in that area were usually hosted by farmers with a big field emptied of cows for the day.

Those days taught us how to have JOY, no matter what.

An additional song on joy is Tommy Walker, on You Tube, Joy, Joy, Joy. Listen to songs about joy with your children. Talk to them. Can they draw pictures of JOY! The younger they are, the more likely they are to draw a great picture of joy without wondering what YOU want from them, or what other adults want from them.

Learn from your children. JOY is a feeling, not a thing. YOU learn to draw it.

*Draw a picture of JOY for yourself. Let go,
be a child again, draw it as you FEEL it.*

Chapter Three

. . . .

JOY

JOY, down in my heart. Gospel song about Joy.

JOY says the Bible, is something God wants each of us to enJOY.

Most religions teach us the exact opposite, in fact teach us that God wants us to suffer until some unknown new day comes in which we ALL will be happy IF we have not broken any of the man made rules which in general keep the PEOPLE from standing up for themselves and DOING what Jesus told us God wants us TO DO, honor GOD and love one another as ourselves.

GOD LOVES ME.

I AM WONDERFUL BECAUSE GOD
CREATED ME.

These are the introductory sentences we
utilize in all of our programs. Some people
find it very hard to say these words. they are
so beaten down by a society that constantly
tells us we are not good enough.

If you find it hard to believe and embrace
these statements, sing the song, and say the
sentences. Write the sentences on placards
and place them around your house, car,
put them on your phone and computer for
opening screens.

Many religions are so concerned with what
THEY do not want you to do, or not do, they
forget to teach us all that loving is about joy,
about patience, about forgiveness.

Chapter Four

. . . .

JOY, in loving ME

IF I love ME, I am likely to be happy. IF I love my children, they are likely to be happy, no matter what, because I will train them to love themselves.

This does not mean any of us are going to be dancing with happiness because of stressful or bad things, it means we are able to see good things around the edges, over the top, under the bad things and have HOPE.

I was teaching Sunday School, and asked to be the interim Sunday School Director for a busy, popular church until they found a new Director.

The first day, I printed out name tags, that said, MY NAME IS............and on the second line, I AM WONDERFUL BECAUSE GOD CREATED ME

When each of us learns to be happy because we are ourselves, unique and created by Creator, we will be on the path to happiness, joy and peace in our lives.

Say these words to yourself, write them on cards, put them around your house......I am wonderful because GOD created me to be unique, to be wonderful

I do not think I know what God has to say, but I would hazard a guess that God does not have the latest trend list and measure us against that list.

I am pretty sure God is NOT looking to see if children have the most popular other children as their boy or girlfriend.

We spend our lives being bombarded, generally from our own parents to start with, with the FACT that we are NOT OK. How does it really look that five year olds think they are ugly because they do not look like forty year old movie or music stars? How does it really look that our children and teens want to walk around in the clothing people wear for their JOBS. Music, drama, making movies are ALL jobs. Help your child realize, if we put every single person working in America on the sides of busses, on billboards, and on commercials EVERYone would be a star!

Learn to look at EVERYONE with God's eyes, how do you see each one. It might be your Mom or Dad, a neighbor, the people who help you at the store, or the doctor's office. Make a list of what God might see in you, and anyone you see along your day.

Make a list of all the "mistakes" God made when creating YOU, the color of your skin, the hair you got, your nose, your voice, do you see where you get these ideas? God is wrong and WHO is right about you.

Chapter Five

· ·

Love down in my heart

Even when I do NOT feel like it, I can go to the love of Jesus down in my heart, even if that is not MY family religion. YOU MIGHT need the love of JESUS for YOU at any moment. If you find that, and give some away, it might help you find your joy again.

Chapter Six

. . . .

Let bad sit on a tack

When things come that make us feel angry, bitter, afraid, mean, alone we can learn to turn those feelings into positive action.

It is HARD, HARD, HARD to face what we know is making us sad, angry, bitter, afraid, mean, or alone. It is HARDER, HARDER, HARDER to learn to face the realities with open eyes, and heart and deal with them. Sadness is hard, especially if it is the death of someone, or a pet that we love. WE as adults have to discover our own inner strength and how to deal so we can teach our children to do the same. We have to discover how to build on OUR inner strength, courage and wisdom on God's gifts to each of us. For those who believe, Jesus helps to reach out and accept that strength, courage and wisdom. AND we need to teach our children how to find and accept this gift.

List problems you have, or things you wish were different so YOU or your child would be OK? Where did you get that idea of not OK-ness

Who is it you let have more power over your OK-ness more than the Creator that made you?

How can you take that power back?

Chapter Seven

Get the Peace that passes all understanding

How do we believe that peace exists, and find it?

How do we share that belief in that inner peace, and help our children and others find it?

Chapter Eight

. . . .

JOY, down in MY heart to stay

Does it mean something is wrong with ME if I lose my peace, my joy, my love? How can I find it again.

NO ONE except you can find your own pathway to joy, or back to it, but we ALL get guidelines in songs, in scriptures and poems and books from people alive, or long passed who have dealt with the same feelings and despair.

What are ways you can remind yourself
that God is always there for you?

What if you do not believe in God as other people around you?

Chapter Nine

. . . .

"Eyes on the sparrow"

Bible: Matthew: 10:31. If he cares so for the sparrow, how much more will he care for YOU?

"he will take good care of me"
gospel song, joy joy joy, Tommy Walker, You Tube.

"I will take your part". Simon and Garfunkel Bridge Over Troubled Waters, You Tube

How do we find the faith, to have joy, to feel good about ourselves, and help our children to have that same faith, and joy, to feel good about themselves and share it with others?

As a mustard seed....Bible Matthew 20;17. Jesus talked about mustard seeds. If we have faith, "as a mustard seed" and ask a mountain to move, with God's help that mountain will move, if we ask with another, in faith, and ask help from God in the way Jesus told us to ask.

Anyone who lived through Mount Saint Helens or any other volcano disaster knows in fact that even mountains DO move, raise up, or disappear, whether some person wanted that particular mountain TO move or NOT at that time, it does show the hugeness of the power of the universe.

Prayer is always answered: Rev. Fred Price Prayer is always answered, but we need to remind ourselves that when dealing with another person, that prayer involves the other person, and that sometimes, just as the answers we give our children, the answer is not now, wait, NO, and sometimes what can we change to make this happen.

God is not a vending Machine: put in prayer, get our what you want...Rev. Zelda Kennedy

Sometimes, just as our children, we ask for things that are not good for us, or are not at this time, or consider the rights of other people, nature and animals.

Chapter Ten

. . . .

Closing

Other books in our programs:

All of our group of books, and workbooks contain some work pages, and/or suggestions for the reader, and those teaching these books to make notes, to go to computer, and libraries and ask others for information to help these projects work their best.

To utilize these to their fullest, make sure YOU model the increased thoughts and availability of more knowledge to anyone you share these books and workbooks with in classes, or community groups.

Magazines are, as noted in most of the books, a wonderful place to look for and find ongoing research and information. Online search engines often bring up new research in the areas, and newly published material.

We all have examples of how we learned and who it was that taught us.

One of the strangest lessons I have learned was walking to a shoot in downtown Los Angeles. The person who kindly told me to park my truck in Pasadena, and take the train had been unaware that the weekend busses did NOT run early in the morning when the crews had to be in to set up. That person, being just a participant, was going much later in the day, taking a taxi, and had no idea how often crews do NOT carry purses with credit cards, large amounts of cash, and have nowhere to carry those items, because the crew works hard, and fast during a set up and tear down and after the shoot are TIRED and not looking to have to find items that have been left around, or stolen.

As I walked, I had to travel through an area of Los Angeles that had become truly run down and many homeless were encamped about and sleeping on the sidewalks and in alleys. I saw a man, that having worked in an ER for many years I realized was DEAD. I used to have thoughts about people who did not notice people needing help, I thought, this poor man, this is probably the most peace he has had in a long time. I prayed for him and went off to my unwanted walk across town. As I walked, I thought about myself, was I just heartless, or was I truly thinking this was the only moment of peace this man had had for a long time and just leaving him to it. What good were upset neighbors, and police, fire trucks and ambulances going to do. He was calmly, eyes open, staring out at a world that had failed him while alive, why rush to disturb him now that nothing could be done.

I did make sure he was DEAD. He was, quite cold rigid.

I learned that day that it is best to do what a person needs, NOT what we need.

Learning is about introspection and grounding of material. Passing little tests on short term memory skills and not knowing what it all means is NOT education, or teaching.

As a high school student, in accelerated Math and Science programs, in which I received 4.0 grades consistently, I walked across a field, diagonally, and suddenly all that math and science made sense, it was not just exercises on paper I could throw answers back on paper, but I realized had NO clue as to what it all really meant.

OTHER BOOKS BY
THIS AUTHOR, AND TEAM

. . . .

Most, if not all, of these books are written at a fourth grade level. FIrst, the author is severely brain damaged from a high fever disease caused by a sample that came in the mail, without a warning that it had killed during test marketing. During the law suit, it was discovered that the corporation had known prior to mailing out ten million samples, WITHOUT warnings of disease and known deaths, and then NOT telling anyone after a large number of deaths around the world started. Second, the target audience is high risk youth, and young veterans, most with a poor education before signing into, or being drafted into the military as a hope Many of our veterans are Vietnam or WWII era.

Maybe those recruiting promises would come true. They would be trained, educated, and given chance for a home, and to protect our country and its principles. Watch the movies Platoon, and Born on the Fourth of July as well as the Oliver Stone series on history to find out how these dreams were meet.

DO NOT bother to write and tell us of grammar or spelling errors. We often wrote these books and workbooks fast for copyrights. We had learned our lessons about giving our material away when one huge charity asked us for our material, promising a grant, Instead, we heard a couple of years later they had built their own VERY similar project, except theirs charged for services, ours were FREE, and theirs was just for a small group, ours was training veterans and others to spread the programs as fast as they could... They got a Nobel Peace prize. We keep saying we are not bitter, we keep saying we did not do our work to get awards, or thousands of dollars of grants....but, it hurts. Especially when lied to and that group STILL sends people to US for help when they can not meet the needs, or the veterans and family can not afford their "charitable" services. One other group had the nerve to send us a Cease and Desist using our own name. We said go ahead and sue, we have proof of legal use of this name for decades. That man had the conscience to apologize, his program was not even FOR veterans or first responders, or their families, nor high risk kids. But we learned. Sometimes life is very unfair.

We got sued again later for the same issue. We settled out of Court as our programs were just restarting and one of the veterans said, let's just change that part of the name and keep on training veterans to run their own programs. Smart young man.

Book List:
The Grandparents Story list will add 12 new titles this year. We encourage every family to write their own historic stories. That strange old Aunt who when you listen to her stories left a rich and well regulated life in the Eastern New York coastal fashionable families to learn Telegraph messaging and go out to the old west to LIVE her life. That old Grandfather or Grandmother who was sent by family in other countries torn by war

to pick up those "dollars in the streets" as noted in the book of that title.

Books in publication, or out by summer 2021

Carousel Horse: A Children's book about equine therapy and what schools MIGHT be and are in special private programs.

Carousel Horse: A smaller version of the original Carousel Horse, both contain the workbooks and the screenplays used for on site stable programs as well as lock down programs where the children and teens are not able to go out to the stables.

Spirit Horse II: This is the work book for training veterans and others interested in starting their own Equine Therapy based programs. To be used as primary education sites, or for supplementing public or private school programs. One major goal of this book is to copyright our founding material, as we gave it away freely to those who said they wanted to help us get grants. They did not. Instead they built their own programs, with grant money, and with donations in small, beautiful stables and won....a Nobel

Peace Prize for programs we invented. We learned our lessons, although we do not do our work for awards, or grants, we DO not like to be ripped off, so now we copyright.

Reassessing and Restructuring Public Agencies; This book is an over view of our government systems and how they were expected to be utilized for public betterment. This is a Fourth Grade level condemnation of a PhD dissertation that was not accepted be because the mentor thought it was "against government"... The first paragraph noted that a request had been made, and referrals given by the then White House.

Reassessing and Restructuring Public Agencies; TWO. This book is a suggestive and creative work to give THE PEOPLE the idea of taking back their government and making the money spent and the agencies running SERVE the PEOPLE ;not politicians. This is NOT against government, it is about the DUTY of the PEOPLE to oversee and control government before it overcomes us.

Could This Be Magic? A Very Short Book. This is a very short book of pictures and the author's personal experiences as the Hall of Fame band VAN HALEN practiced in her garage. The pictures are taken by the author, and her then five year old son. People wanted copies of the pictures, and permission was given to publish them to raise money for treatment and long term Veteran homes.

Carousel TWO: Equine therapy for Veterans. publication pending 2021

Carousel THREE: Still Spinning: Special Equine therapy for women veterans and single mothers. This book includes TWELVE STEPS BACK FROM BETRAYAL for soldiers who have been sexually assaulted in the active duty military and help from each other to heal, no matter how horrible the situation. publication pending 2021

LEGAL ETHICS: AN OXYMORON. A book to give to lawyers and judges you feel have not gotten the justice of American Constitution based law (Politicians are great persons to gift with this book). Publication late 2021

PARENTS CAN LIVE and raise great kids.

Included in this book are excerpts from our workbooks from KIDS ANONYMOUS and KIDS JR, and A PARENTS PLAIN RAP (to teach sexuality and relationships to their children. This program came from a copyrighted project thirty years ago, which has been networked into our other programs. This is our training work book. We asked AA what we had to do to become a real Twelve Step program as this is considered a quasi twelve step program children and teens can use to heal BEFORE becoming involved in drugs, sexual addiction, sexual trafficking and relationship woes, as well as unwanted, neglected and abused or having children murdered by parents not able to deal with the reality of parenting. Many of our original students were children of abuse and neglect, no matter how wealthy. Often the neglect was by society itself when children lost parents to illness, accidents or addiction. We were told, send us a copy and make sure you call it quasi. The Teens in the first programs when surveyed for the outcome research reports said, WE NEEDED THIS EARLIER. SO they helped younger children invent KIDS JR. Will be republished in 2021 as a documentary of the work and success of these projects.

Addicted To Dick. This is a quasi Twelve Step program for women in domestic violence programs mandated by Courts due to repeated incidents and danger, or actual injury or death of their children.

Addicted to Dick 2018 This book is a specially requested workbook for women in custody, or out on probation for abuse to their children, either by themselves or their sexual partners or spouses. The estimated national number for children at risk at the time of request was three million across the nation. During Covid it is estimated that number has risen. Homelessness and undocumented families that are unlikely to be reported or found are creating discussion of a much larger number of children maimed or killed in these domestic violence crimes. THE most important point in this book is to force every local school district to train teachers, and all staff to recognize children at risk, and to report their family for HELP, not punishment. The second most important part is to teach every child on American soil to know to ask for help, no matter that parents, or other relatives or known adults, or unknown adults have threatened to kill them for "telling". Most, if not all paramedics, emergency rooms, and police and fire stations are trained to protect the children and teens, and get help for the family... PUNISHMENT is not the goal, eliminating childhood abuse and injury or death at the hands of family is the goal of all these projects. In some areas JUDGES of child and family courts were taking training and teaching programs themselves to HELP. FREE...

Addicted to Locker Room BS. This book is about MEN who are addicted to the lies told in locker rooms and bars. During volunteer work at just one of several huge juvenile lock downs, where juveniles who have been convicted as adults, but are waiting for their 18th birthday to be sent to adult prisons, we noticed that the young boys and teens had "big" ideas of themselves, learned in locker rooms and back alleys. Hundreds of these young boys would march, monotonously around the enclosures, their lives over. often facing long term adult prison sentences.

The girls, we noticed that the girls, for the most part were smart, had done well in school, then "something" happened. During the years involved in this volunteer work I saw only ONE young girl who was so mentally ill I felt she was not reachable, and should be in a locked down mental health facility for help; if at all possible, and if teachers, and others had been properly trained, helped BEFORE she gotten to that place, lost in the horror and broken of her childhood and early teen years.

We noticed that many of the young women in non military sexual assault healing programs were "betrayed" in many ways, by step fathers, boyfriends, even fathers, and mothers by either molestation by family members, or allowing family members or friends of parents to molest these young women, often as small children. We asked military sexually assaulted young women to begin to volunteer to help in the programs to heal the young girls and teens, it helped heal them all.

There was NOTHING for the boys that even began to reach them until our research began on the locker room BS theory of life destruction and possible salvaging by the boys themselves, and men in prisons who helped put together something they thought they MIGHT have heard before they ended up in prison.

Americans CAN Live Happily Ever After. Parents edition.One

Americans CAN Live Happily Ever After. Children's edition Two.

Americans CAN Live Happily Ever After. Three. After Covid. This book includes "Welcome to America" a requested consult workbook for children and youth finding themselves in cages, auditoriums on cots, or in foster group homes or foster care of relatives or non-relatives with NO guidelines for their particular issues. WE ASKED the kids, and they helped us write this fourth grade level workbook portion of this book to help one another and each other. Written in a hurry! We were asked to use our expertise in other youth programs, and our years of experience teaching and working in high risk youth programs to find something to help.

REZ CHEESE Written by a Native American /WASP mix woman. Using food, and thoughts on not getting THE DIABETES, stories are included of a childhood between two worlds.

REZ CHEESE TWO A continuation of the stress on THE DIABETES needing treatment and health care from birth as well as recipes, and stories from Native America, including thoughts on asking youth to help stop the overwhelming numbers of suicide by our people.

BIG LIZ: LEADER OF THE GANG Stories of unique Racial Tension and Gang Abatement projects created when gangs and racial problems began to make schools unsafe for our children.

DOLLARS IN THE STREETS, ghost edited for author Lydia Caceras, the first woman horse trainer at Belmont Park.

95 YEARS of TEACHING:

A book on teaching, as opposed to kid flipping

Two teachers who have created and implemented systems for private and public education a combined 95 plus years of teaching talk about experiences and realities and how parents can get involved in education for their children. Included are excerpts from our KIDS ANONYMOUS and KIDS JR workbooks of over 30 years of free youth programs.

A HORSE IS NOT A BICYCLE. A book about pet ownership and how to prepare your children for responsible pet ownership and along the way to be responsible parents. NO ONE needs to own a pet, or have a child, but if they make that choice, the animal, or child deserves a solid, caring forever home.

OLD MAN THINGS and MARE'S TALES. this is a fun book about old horse trainers I met along the way. My husband used to call the old man stories "old man things", which are those enchanting and often very effective methods of horse, pet, and even child rearing. I always said I brought up my children and my students the same as I had trained horses and dogs......I meant that horses and dogs had taught me a lot of sensible, humane ways to bring up an individual, caring, and dream realizing adult who was HAPPY and loved.

STOP TALKING, DO IT

ALL of us have dreams, intentions, make promises. This book is a workbook from one of our programs to help a person make their dreams come true, to build their intentions into goals, and realities, and to keep their promises. One story from this book, that inspired the concept is a high school kid, now in his sixties, that was in a special ed program for drug abuse and not doing well in school. When asked, he said his problem was that his parents would not allow him to buy a motorcycle. He admitted that he did not have money to buy one, insure one, take proper driver's education and licensing examinations to own one, even though he had a job. He was asked to figure out how much money he was spending on drugs. Wasting his own money, stealing from his parents and other relatives, and then to figure out, if he saved his own money, did some side jobs for neighbors and family until he was 18, he COULD afford the motorcycle and all it required to legally own one. In fact, he did all, but decided to spend the money on college instead of the motorcycle when he graduated from high school. His priorities had changed as he learned about responsible motorcycle ownership and risk doing the assignments needed for his special ed program. He also gave up drugs, since his stated reason was he could not have a motorcycle, and that was no longer true, he COULD have a motorcycle, just had to buy it himself, not just expect his parents to give it to him.

Printed in the United States
by Baker & Taylor Publisher Services